"Oral Sex Because Satis

ORAL SEX MADE SIMPLE

A NO-NONSENSE GUIDE TO P*SSY EATING

Katie Caroline

TABLE OF CONTENTS

INTRODUCTION

Pussy can be well eaten by any dinosaur, male or female, or unicorn but for women and other individuals with vaginas, eating pussy, licking out, going down on someone, eating someone out, or whatever you want to call oral sex may be a lot of fun.

Cunnilingus concentrates on stimulating the clitoris, which gives a lot of pleasure (often more so than penetration).

In fact, oral sex is frequently regarded as the most reliable method of delivering the big O to a vulva. The majority of vulva owners require clitoral stimulation to attain orgasm, and oral sex puts the clit in the spotlight.

This book is great as a personal guidebook or a present because it does more than just spice up your life or the lives of others; it helps to transform everything for the better.

For most women, sex, especially oral sex, is a source of great pleasure, as they can achieve orgasm with direct clitoral stimulation. Your cunnilingus abilities will come in helpful here. It's not just a skill; it can also transform you into the best she's ever had.

Do you want to know how to blow her mind when you're showing her some love? You've come to the proper book if that's the case.

THE 7 STEP BUILD-UP TO BE AWARE OF

If you put in the easy and enjoyable effort after ensuring the mood, timing, and place are all perfect, foreplay increases the likelihood that she will climax by 50%.

Now, here's how to tease her step by step:

1. Start with a soft kiss from her mouth to her breasts. As you approach her waist and hips, continue kissing her body. As you approach her underwear, place a hand on each leg and slowly spread them out. Erogenous zones are sensitive regions on a woman's body that get her on - and you might be surprised by some of them!

2. Panties - Don't bother removing her panties for the time being. Instead, kiss her vulva/vagina through them, gently squeezing it with your lips. You can also delicately glide

your tongue over her vagina from bottom to clit.

3. Lower - Move your kissing along her inner thigh to a lower place after kissing her through her underwear for a few minutes. You can go up to the inside of her knee here, but the more you get away from her vaginal area, the less sensitive it becomes. Kiss her down her inner thigh with one leg, then switch to the other leg.

Softly grab the flesh of her inner thigh between your lips or perhaps your teeth, but not too forcefully, if she prefers it a little tougher. If you don't, you run the risk of seriously harming her. You can even suck the skin to give her an unnoticeable hickey.

As you move to the opposite leg, spend a little more time licking her vagina outside of her underpants. If she wants you to start eating her out at this point, don't be surprised...if she does, go slow to keep the anticipation going.

4. Before removing her panties, move your way over her clit to the top of her underwear and give her some delicate kisses on her mons (the area above her clitoris).

5. Place your fingers on either side of her underpants, on the outside of her hips, and slowly pull them down until they're fully off if she hasn't done so previously.

6. Close Call - Gently kiss and lick her vagina and clit all over (very softly). As you move around, the edge of your lips should make a slight contact with her vagina and clit...teasing her all the time.

7. The Big Course — Now it's time for the main event... It's time to start using the Pancake and Vortex to create the most extreme orgasms, which we'll go through in the following chapters.

MASTERING THE TECHNIQUE OF PANCAKES

This approach is simple to utilize and, as previously said, will provide her with the most intense orgasms possible while eating out her pussy. It's insanely simple to create a PANCAKE.

To begin, take your tongue out of your mouth. Allow it to fall down your chin to relax you. Now is the time to make it wide and flat (like a pancake).

You'll be holding your tongue in this position while performing the Pancake, keeping it relaxed, broad, and flat.

To do the Pancake, start with the base of your tongue at the bottom of her vulva. Slowly raise your head from the bottom of her vagina to the top, allowing your tongue to glide from the bottom to the top, passing over her clit.

Make sure you don't move your tongue. Maintain a relaxed, broad, and flat demeanor. Instead, your head will be in charge of every movement. As your head raises, your tongue will rise with it.

Come to a halt when you reach the top, draw away from her until you are no longer in contact, and then start over from the bottom.

Maintaining a relaxed, broad, and flat tongue helps you to cover as much of her vulva/vagina as possible, giving her the greatest feeling imaginable.

When it comes to performing the Pancake, that's all there is to it...

There are a few things to keep in mind, but...

When I raise my head, what am I supposed to do with my tongue?

Simply keep it flat and loose. It's as simple as that. It's best not to try to make any shapes with it. It shouldn't be curled up in any way.

Make no flicking motions with your hand. Remember that when you're eating out with your girl, your tongue should be relaxed and flat.

How much pressure should I apply to eat pussy properly?

To begin, you won't use your tongue muscles to exert pressure as you move upwards in the Pancake because you'll be concentrating on keeping it relaxed and flat.

If I sound like a broken record, it's because this is crucial to remember.

Your head and neck will be used to apply pressure. This prevents your tongue from being weary, allowing you to perform cunnilingus for longer periods of time while also allowing you to apply tremendous amounts of pressure (if required).

So, how much pressure should you use?

The smallest amount possible When there's more strain on the body, orgasms aren't always more intense. For the first few minutes, apply gentle pressure to watch how she reacts. You should be so light that you don't even come close to making contact with her.

If she can climax with very little pressure, you should only use little pressure.

If she doesn't react much (faster breathing, moaning, grabbing linens, bodily tension indicating she's about to climax), gently raise the pressure until you can see she's having enjoyment. However, as you're eating her out, your goal should always be to apply the least amount of pressure possible to induce her to cum.

This has to do with the amount of pressure you use.

As much as possible, slow down.

You'll have to see how she responds to this. If she isn't enjoying your gradual movement, you'll need to increase up the pace. Many women can cum when you softly glide from the bottom to the top of their vaginal canal over 15 long, delicious seconds, but others demand that you move as swiftly as a dog drinking water!

When deciding how much pressure to use and how rapidly you should move, pay attention to her body and how she reacts. You should also seek her advice on your strategy. Don't be afraid to ask her whether she's having a good time.

You might also test the waters by informing her you'll be trying out a few different approaches and asking her to rate them.

Is there anything I should do differently while she's on the verge of giving birth?

There are two schools of thought when it comes to what to do when she is ready to cum. The first is for beginners and intermediates, while the second is for those with more experience.

(beginning-intermediate)   Super-Constant Speed – If you're trying to make them cum, most girls prefer it if you can hold a very steady pace. As a result, maintain the same level of pressure and pace. Changing things up now could ruin her orgasm and her mood.

Agonizing Slow Down (advanced) - If you've ever gone down on your girl and made her orgasm, the Agonizing Slow Down is for you.

Here's how to get started...

When you feel that she is approaching climax, slow down slightly so that the last approach to orgasm takes longer than usual. This way, she'll be able to savor the hyper-pleasant build-up to orgasm for a longer period of time.

Slow down the closer she gets to climax, and as you do this more and more, she'll be able to appreciate that incredibly strong feeling right before her eyes. Her cum will be much more difficult than usual as a result of this. You won't be accustomed with how her body reacts to your tongue if you haven't eaten her pussy before. If you're new to sucking her pussy, the Agonizing Slow Down is a surefire way to make her frustrated and unsatisfied.

Is there anything I should do AFTER the orgasm?

Most women, like men, go through a refraction phase when they have clitoral orgasms. When her clitoris and vulva are touched, they become incredibly sensitive, and it causes them agony.

So, what should you do if your partner is having a refractory period?

Obviously, leave it alone for a few minutes!

Instead, focus your attention on other areas of her body, such as her vaginal area and inner thighs. Make every effort to avoid coming into contact with her clit and vulva. Returning to foreplay or simply lying next to her till she recovers are other alternatives.

You can test her sensitivity by kissing the bottom of her vagina and observing her reaction after a minute or two if you want to keep eating her out (and she wants it). If she flinches, wait a little longer. If she likes it, raise your tongue to the point where you can touch her clit.

You'll have to wait a little longer if she flinches on your way up.

STYLING IN THE VORTEX MANNER

The Vortex is simple to use and effective at rolling her eyes back.

Make a small "O" shape with your lips. This "O" should be about the same size as her clitoral region.

Make sure your lips are covered with saliva as you place this "O" over your girl's clit and the surrounding area.

Then start sucking it slowly.

Her clitus will be dragged up into your mouth, which she will find quite pleasurable.

That's the basic method, but you should try out different variations while keeping track of what she likes best.

Constant Vortex - The simplest way to conduct the Vortex is to maintain a constant level of suction. Some ladies only need this to reach climax.

Rhythmic Vortex - In a rhythmic pattern, you'll be sucking and releasing pressure, bringing her clit in and out of your mouth and releasing it. How quickly you complete this is entirely up to you.

It can be played as slowly as a slow song or as swiftly as the beat of an upbeat song. Find out what she enjoys by talking to her or observing her body language.

Hard Vortex, Slow Release - Apply a strong amount of suction to her clit quickly, then slowly release it. As needed, rinse and repeat.

Suck her clit into your mouth and keep it there while rubbing her clit with your tongue (my favorite). As previously stated, try varying the speed and pressure with which you lick her to determine what she prefers.

I'm not sure how big I should make my O.

The solution to this question is...

Whatever method is most efficient.

Go ahead and give your girl a small "O," where you can barely take her clit into your lips. Do it instead if she likes it when you suck in her clit, labia, and vulva with a big "O."

Listen to her body for signs, but also chat to her, and you'll figure out just what she need for her most passionate orgasms.

Should I use my teeth to chomp on her clit?

Certainly not! Your teeth are quite likely to cause her clit pain because it is one of her most sensitive body parts. You must proceed with utmost caution, even if she directly demands it, and I strongly advise against using your teeth.

This is the only pussy eating strategy you'll ever need to deliver mind-altering orgasms to your girl and make you the best she's ever known.

7 EXTREMELY EFFECTIVE PUSSY EATING TECHNIQUES

Of course, there are other cunnilingus methods for keeping things fresh, even if they aren't as effective as the Pancake & Vortex...

So, if you've developed a habit or have become too predictable when it comes to licking and sucking her pussy, you might want to try some of the following ideas...

1. Putting Pressure

This method comprises applying greater pressure on the area just beneath her clitoris during the Pancake.

Increase the pressure as you make your way up her vulva to the point where the base of your tongue is pinched beneath her clit.

Slowly lower your tongue till the base of your tongue is pressed against her clit, but don't ease up on the pressure.

As you ascend, the texture of your tongue will stimulate the bottom of her clit, giving your oral sex abilities a new dimension.

2. Take Her To The Edge And Back

Edging is a good way to make her orgasms louder. The best part is that you don't have to wait until you're about to devour her alive to use your edging. You can use it to climax her during anal sex, regular intercourse, or any other activity.

We'll talk about how to edge her while licking her pussy for the time being.

Begin by devouring her as you normally would.

When you see she's getting close to climaxing, slow down and back off so she doesn't orgasm.

Spend 20 to 5 minutes doing anything fun that won't make her orgasm, like:

• Kissing her vaginal region from top to bottom.

• Kissing her on the thighs' insides.

• Keeping your attention fixed on her breasts.

When she has calmed down a little, you can resume eating her out as normal, but at a somewhat slower pace this time. You should maintain repeating this until she's ready to climax, at which point you should... halt.

Wait till she has calmed down before doing something else sweet but non-orgasm-inducing.

Start eating her out again, but this time at a more leisurely pace, until she succumbs.

I'm almost certain that edging her this way will result in one of, if not the most, powerful orgasms of her life.

Edging can also be utilized during any orgasm-inducing activity, as I previously said.

Some women may find it tough to come even if you eat pussy adequately. If you find yourself in this circumstance, I don't recommend trying this strategy because you'll both be frustrated.

3. Give your index finger to her.

It might be a lot of fun to devour her pussy with your fingers. It allows you to provide her with more stimulation, thrills her both internally and outwardly, and gives her a variety of stimulation options. Fingering her while eating her out can be done in a variety of ways, some of which are simple and others which are exceedingly tough.

4. Finger Her G Spot & Lick Her Clit

It's a good idea to lick her clit or use the Beneath Pressure method of providing extra pressure under her clit while fingering her G Spot. Oral and physical sex (fingering), as well as deep kissing, are the three activities most likely to turn a woman off, according to studies. As a result, your oral sex abilities may be more crucial than you realize.

Externally, you can stimulate the G-spot by pressing down with your free hand on her mons pubis. Some girls like it when you massage this part of their body.

5. Finger the Vaginal Bottom and Suck Her Clit

While doing so, try stroking the bottom of her vaginal canal as deeply as possible.

Keep in mind that while the bottom of some women's vaginas aren't particularly sensitive, the bottom of their vaginas at the back are. You might have trouble reaching it unless you have extremely long fingers. You can always use a dildo or penis-shaped vibrator instead of your finger if you have one.

6. Lick Her Clit, Play With Her Ass, Finger Her G Spot

If it's not too strange or uncomfortable for her, you can use the other hand to rub her ass while your tongue is concentrated on her clit.

There are various ways to have a good time with her ass.

• Massage it just on the outside, never on the inside.

• Gently press down on the opening with mild, rhythmic pressure, but don't penetrate it.

• Penetrating both inside and outside the building.

• Using your finger to squeeze her ass (s).

Note: The simplest way to play with her ass is to put your arm over her leg and reach around from behind.

Warning: Do not touch her vagina with one or both hands after using them on her ass. You run the risk of infecting her vaginal area if you do.

7. Experiment

I've given you a few ideas on how to lick her pussy with your fingers, but there are so many more alternatives. While eating her out, you don't even need to use your fingers. You may, for example, finger her to stop licking her pussy and then continue when you're ready.

7 ADDITIONAL WAYS TO GET HER TO MARS

Eating pussy is a serious undertaking. Don't worry, I've got some further advice for you. It's fine if you want to eat some popcorn while you read. Let's continue:

1. The Game of Power

When you're eating her pussy out, a little power-play might be pretty enticing. There are two ways to do this:

Tying her arms above her head before you lick her out will be a lot of fun for both of you if your girl like being restricted while you're intimate. It deprives her of a lot of her authority.

Encourage Her to Take Charge - She might enjoy being the boss.

She might take authority by putting her hands on your head while you're eating her pussy. She will be able to regulate your position, pace, and pressure as you eat her out.

If you're not careful, she'll grab your hair and force her crotch against your face (winks!).

It's so much fun to watch women devour pussy... (Just putting it out there!!!)

This also allows her to push your head away if her clit becomes too sensitive after the climax.

2. Encourage her to lend a hand.

Pussy eating is a team activity that may be enjoyed by both men and women. This is especially true if your girl struggles to achieve orgasm.

If your girl is unable to cum while you suck her pussy, she may use her hands to provide more stimulation. She may also spread her labia out of the way, allowing you to kiss and suck her pussy while she does so.

She can even express her wants by asking you to exert more or less pressure, go quicker or slower, or refocus your efforts in a different manner.

3. Experiment With Your Tongue

I know I stated at the beginning of this pussy eating school that you don't have to move your tongue or flick it when you're eating her.

This is right for the most part...but...

It's not a bad idea to give it a shot and see how she reacts. Many women find it more irritating than pleasurable to have their clits flicked mercilessly by the tip of their tongue.

However, it is enjoyed by a tiny percentage of women, and some may prefer it as a parting gesture...

It's also a great way to change things up now and again. You might want to take a look at:

• Curling your tongue and using it to pierce her.

• Twirling her clitoral region with your tongue.

• Changing the position of her clitus up and down and side to side.

• Flipping the Pancake the other way around. Start at the top and work your way down her clit.

• You may even try to keep her pussy in place by putting constant pressure to it.

4. Pick a side and stick with it.

Choose which side of her clit she prefers to be rubbed!

Which side is preferable: the left or right?

Is it better to start from the top or at the bottom?

Is there a happy medium?

On each side of her vaginal entrance, the clitoris' crura (legs) extend below the clitoris and beneath the skin. This could explain why one side of her body is more sensitive than the other.

5. The warmer the weather, the better.

This is more of a guide than a method for going down or learning how to finger a woman. If you can get it as wet as possible, it will feel better for your girl.

I'm not talking about water usage.

Rather, I'm talking about squeezing out as much saliva as possible. Also, if you have trouble producing enough saliva, I strongly recommend that you use lubrication instead. Flavored lube might also help you enjoy the sport more.

6. 'Cool Runnings' is a film that

Drawback and form the same "O" shape with your lips as you did during the Vortex if you want to take a break from licking her pussy.

Then gently blow on her moist pussy to give her a cooling sensation.

This is also a great maneuver to do when her clit and vulva are too sensitive to touch during her refractory phase.

7. Consume Her Ass

Eating her ass after you eat her pussy is fantastic if she likes anilingus.

Warning: Don't touch her pussy again until your hands are thoroughly cleansed after touching her anus with your mouth. Small amounts of dangerous germs are almost certainly present in your mouth (no matter how clean she is). Your mouth's dangerous bacteria can then reach her vaginal area, causing discomfort and illness.

If you lick her anus, you don't want to go back to tongue stimulation in vaginal stimulation.

MOST EATERS MAKE 11 DANGEROUS MISTAKES

Unfortunately, there are a number of potential obstacles and roadblocks that may limit the amount of pleasure you can give your girl while licking her pussy. You must be aware of these concerns and take steps to avoid them if you want to get the most out of your pussy eating efforts.

1. Don't Use the Letters - This is where you use your tongue to draw the alphabet on her clit/pussy. Most females dislike it when you spell the alphabet with your tongue on their pussy.

Due to its severe unpredictability, this strategy is unsuccessful. You might pay a visit to a sweet area she enjoys, but you won't stay long.

2. Consistency is essential — being inconsistent can upset your girl and make orgasming tough for her. Most males feel the same way about getting a hand job/blow job, for example. It's aggravating when they're stroked at odd intervals.

In other words, even if she's ready to cum, you should try to maintain the same rhythm, tempo, and pressure when you go down on her.

3. Listen for Feedback - Horrible partners aren't interested in hearing what others have to say about them. You must pay close attention to her reaction, both in terms of how her body reacts and in terms of actively asking her what she values most.

As you gain more insight from her, you'll be able to build up a mental library of methods, and you'll be able to persuade her that you're the best lover she's ever had.

You're doing a good job if she's groaning or sounds out of breath; keep listening to her body; if she shuts her eyes, tenses her body, or begins breathing faster/harder, she's clearly on the verge of orgasm, and all you have to do now is keep continuing at the same rate.

On the other side, some women enjoy oral sex but never move beyond it. Learning that not every woman will orgasm or even want to orgasm is an important part of knowing how to offer cunnilingus, as is understanding that you shouldn't rush or pressure her. Knowing how to give cunnilingus requires this knowledge.

4. It's Not a Good Idea to Eat — licking cream off your partner's body can be quite sensual and interesting. Suctioning it from her pussy, on the other hand, could result in serious difficulties.

Some food particles may find their way into the vaginal area, causing irritation, a yeast infection, or even worse (try learning more about yeast infections). As a result, avoid putting cream, chocolate sauce, or anything else on or around her vaginal area.

5. Attempting to replicate pornography during sex, such as fingering or eating her pussy, is almost always a bad idea. Pornography is filmed only for the purpose of making it appear lovely on screen.

Pornographers are worried about whether the performers are having a good time, thus porn isn't the best way to learn proper pussy eating methods.

6. Don't be too harsh with the Clitoris; it's really delicate, so you don't need a lot of force. Although some women enjoy being pushed to their limits, this is not true for everyone.

If she's too sensitive for direct contact, try licking through her jeans.

7. Do Not Try to Recreate Sex - You'll notice that licking her clitoris and vulva is a common theme among the techniques we offer. While many women enjoy vaginal sex, you're limited in what you can do with your tongue, which can't penetrate very far.

Even if you could, the tongue in vagina technique is useless for many women.

You can lick your way through the aperture, and you might even appreciate the taste of her there, but you must return to her clitoris as soon as possible.

Of course, some girls prefer tongue insertion when dining out, so just in case, you should ask. You'll never comprehend how to eat out a female if you're terrified of conversation!

8. Use Your Hands - It's fine to use your hands to finger her pussy. It's also a terrific method to relax your mouth and tongue while also shaking things up, as I previously indicated. After all, variety is the spice of life.

Here are some suggestions for getting your hands dirty.

• You can alternate between stimulating her solely with your tongue, solely with your hands, solely with your tongue, solely with your tongue, solely with your tongue, solely with your tongue, solely with your tongue, solely with your tongue, solely with your tongue, solely with your tongue, solely with your

• You can use both your tongue and your fingers at the same time.

• You can almost fully rely on your hands, and when she approaches a climax, all you need is your tongue to finish her off. Alternatively, the reverse is true.

9. Don't Rush, But Don't Forget Quickies – I've already talked about how taking your

time to build suspense can be really successful.

It simply implies that when you finally go down on her, she'll be so sensitive and prepared that you won't be able to make a mistake.

If you're both at a party and you go away and eat her out before returning knowing you've both been up to no good, it might get pretty steamy.

By switching things up, the idea is to keep things interesting. It would become monotonous for both of you if you keep doing the same thing.

And if you're the type who quickly eats someone out as a form of foreplay before going on to the "other thing," you're missing out — and your girl knows it. If you want to eat pussy like a pro, you must understand that attitude is everything. Do it for the love of it, or at the very least learn to enjoy it.

10. Do seek help - In an ideal world, you'd be able to listen to and monitor your girl's body while experimenting with different approaches on her, allowing you to figure out what works and what doesn't.

Even when orgasming, some women are quieter and may not respond as strongly as others. As a result, determining whether she is having fun or not may be tough.

The only way to remedy this dilemma is for her to provide some feedback. Inquire about what she enjoyed, what she didn't like, and what she would like you to do differently once you've descended on her.

If you do it this way, you'll just get better at eating her out.

11. Make orgasm a secondary goal - doesn't it feel great when she puts her hands on you? The same is true when you look down on her. For some women, achieving an orgasm may be challenging.

In fact, most women report that orgasm is easier to achieve when masturbating alone.

So, don't just focus on making her cum when you're eating her pussy.

It's not a good idea to tell her you're going to help her cum, especially if you've never done so before.

This frees her to simply enjoy the sensation even if she doesn't get off, and she won't feel pressured to fake an orgasm if she doesn't show up.

CONCLUSION

Some women will just reject some of the cunnilingus advice I've just given you, but it doesn't mean she's a bad person. It just means that you should put in more effort to learn about her preferences.

If she has no idea what she likes but enjoys it when you eat her out, I suggest trying a couple different ways to eat her pussy and having her rate them.

In this game, there are no winners or losers; the purpose is to be satisfied.

Notes

Notes

Notes

_____
_____
_____
_____
_____
_____
_____
_____
_____
_____
_____
_____
_____
_____
_____
_____
_____
_____
_____

Notes

Notes

Notes

_____

_____

_____

_____

_____

_____

_____

_____

_____

_____

_____

_____

_____

_____

_____

_____

_____

_____

_____

_____

Notes

Notes

_____

_____

_____

_____

_____

_____

_____

_____

_____

_____

_____

_____

_____

_____

_____

_____

_____

_____

_____

_____

Notes

_____
_____
_____
_____
_____
_____
_____
_____
_____
_____
_____
_____
_____
_____
_____
_____
_____
_____
_____

Notes

_____
_____
_____
_____
_____
_____
_____
_____
_____
_____
_____
_____
_____
_____
_____
_____
_____
_____
_____
_____
_____

Notes

_____
_____
_____
_____
_____
_____
_____
_____
_____
_____
_____
_____
_____
_____
_____
_____
_____
_____
_____
_____

Notes

_____
_____
_____
_____
_____
_____
_____
_____
_____
_____
_____
_____
_____
_____
_____
_____
_____
_____

Made in the USA
Las Vegas, NV
15 March 2024

87233547R00036